SHORTS

Poems and Short Stories

Charles Lopez Bruns

While every precaution has been taken in the preparation of this book, the publisher assumes no responsibility for errors or omissions, or for damages resulting from the use of the information contained herein.

SHORTS: POEMS AND SHORT STORIES
First edition: November 2025
Copyright © 2025 Charles A. Bruns
ISBN: 978-1-7377980-3-3
Written by Charles Lopez Bruns
Published by Charles Anthony Communication
All rights reserved
Media and permissions:
CharlesAnthonyComm@gmail.com
Library of Congress Control Number: 2025921171

Table of Contents

Poems:

<u>Poems by Charles Lopez Bruns</u>

On a Moffitt's Day

On a beautiful Moffitt's evening the full orange
moon
was caressed with the soft edges of adoring clouds.
Lightning drills were confined
to the inside of a white cloud in the distance.
And silence fell early and swiftly
as boats and cars turned in for the night.

With the aroma of a Cohiba and citronella candles,
the scene drew my family out and kept the
mosquitos away,
But only for so long.
Nature always stakes its territory,
forcing us inside to old Tom Waits songs
and the view of flickering campfires in the
darkening night.

In my sleep and in cities hundreds of miles away,
leather shoes and basketballs pound the pavement
and immigrants drink from America and the World
Cup.
I think of the beach, the clear lake, the mountains,
all in view with a cafe con leche in the morning.
I dream of walks around the sites and rides on jet
skis.

On a beautiful Moffitt's morning the clouds and sun
have their daily joust for supremacy,
the clouds with speed and mass on their side,
and the sun with patience and light to boast.
The sun will win today, for the clouds have already
done so
too many other days this week, and we're on
vacation.

A fisherman checks his nets and launches his boat
with the hope of catching dinner for family and
friends.
He, too, will win today, for there are plenty of fish
and they are hungry, just like the campers
and other vacationers in Moffitt's with appetites
for the simple and good things in life.

Written in 1998,
posted on 1400 Characters blog in 2012

LeBron James, pollo grande

He passed up the opportunity to be a New York
hero,
the king of the great city,
perhaps to avoid the pressure cooker.
Instead, he'll stand for the Heat in Miami,
where it may be a lot cooler than Hell's Kitchen.

His face won't be on a large billboard on Times
Square,
and he'll never ride in the Thanksgiving Day
parade,
or have a sandwich named after him by an 8th
Avenue deli.
But, there will be a new set of jerseys
with his name available for sale,
he'll be welcomed in chic South Beach clubs…
and the locals may even create a big chicken
sandwich for him.

"Is that, is that…James LeBron?" a Miamian will
ask.
"He's so big!"
"Yes, yes, it's him. I'm going to name a chicken
sandwich after him.
I'll call it the…James LeBron *pollo grande*.
Maybe he will come in and buy one,
and my sales will increase."

Why would a budding 25-year-old legend pass up
the chance
to play 40-50 games a year at the mecca of

basketball?
Would someone with ambition settle for someone
else's place,
and page three of the sports section in his new
town?
It's puzzling to New Yorkers,
but they're getting over it at a typically fast speed.

Miami is getting over it, too.
It's not hard when its sports fans don't get on to it in
the first place,
their minds already on Hurricanes and Dolphins.
Except for a few of those cafes and sandwich
shops.
"Have a James LeBron *pollo grande* --
it's not cheap, but it's big."

Written and posted on 1400 Characters blog in
2010

The sound of music

In New York City, the streets are filled with the
sound of music.
Walking west of 5th Avenue on 46 Street,
lunchtime,
the sound of Billy Joel could be heard clearly.
Same songs, same voice, same band.
But it was a different guy, with different musicians,
sounding better than the Piano Man himself
probably would today.

Same spot, two weeks earlier,
bunch of guys played music without instruments.
They sang, thumped a beat, kept harmony,
with the help of a tape loop that provided backing
music.
But the tape was the same guys thumping a beat,
keeping harmony, with only their mouths as
instruments.

East and up a few blocks, a couple days earlier,
a larger ensemble of older guys with a woman,
entertained a lunchtime crowd with…
Jazz? Ragtime? American standards?
Perhaps – but feel-good music, definitely.
Passerby saint who came marching in,
heading west on 51 Street in no hurry,
danced to it with a big smile on his face.

Of course, Lady Gaga also graced midtowners

with her presence of a present of a performance
at Rockefeller Center Plaza earlier in the summer,
as did the window-pane rattling Irish rockers
The Script and others on the NBC Today show.

Last December, a Mexican man on guitar and
woman on accordion,
sang a few songs under matching black fedoras on
the F train,
collected a few dollars and hopped off at the next
stop,
exchanging Christmas cheer with riders.

San Juan Hill, where Amsterdam Houses stand,
was also alive with the sound of music back in the
1960s.
Puerto Rican doo-woopers crooned in harmony for
passing neighbors,
even for little boys who listened but pretended not
to see.
In midtown today, only the age of the listener is
different.

*Written and posted on 1400 Characters blog in
2010*

An artistic mission

She jumped inside the taxi
both relieved and tense.
Snow was falling in Long Branch
at the end of a long train ride,
and the station was bustling
with people walking,
cleaning off their cars,
or looking for their ride home.

"How long will it take to
get to Asbury Park?" she asked.
"Where?" the driver asked.
"717 Cookman Avenue,
the Parlor Gallery," she quickly answered.
"Hmm, maybe 20 minutes --
it's hard to know because of the snow,"
the driver answered.

Concerned, she looked at the
two other passengers and asked,
"Should I take a train?"

"Hmm, this is probably faster,"
one fellow passenger replied.
"The train makes a couple of
other stops before getting to
Asbury Park,

and then you have to walk."

The taxi moved slowly
out of the station.
She looked up and asked,
"Should I get my own cab?"
"That's probably not an option
at this point," the other passenger said.
"This isn't Broadway in New York."

"By the time we get there,
I'm going to have only ten minutes
to see the exhibit," she said.
"I was hoping to have more time,
but the train was delayed."

The fellow passenger encouraged her
to enjoy dinner at one of
Asbury Park's fine restaurants,
near the art gallery.
Her response after a silent pause
was simply to inquire whether
the Asbury Park train station had
an indoor seating area.

The taxi continued south
on Ocean Avenue,
preparing to drop off
the first person who,

before wishing his
fellow passengers well,
asked the woman:

"What artist could make someone want
to ride a train for almost two hours
just to see their work for ten minutes?"
"Jill Ricci"

*Written and posted on 1400 Characters blog in
2013*

The bicycle rack

They're built by people in shops around the world,
often by those who use them for daily
transportation.
They're shipped to ports in different countries,
and sold in stores in cities, towns and villages.

Some buy them to get to work every day,
others to do their shopping and errands.
Some have them to get serious exercise,
others for leisurely rides through scenic paths.

Bicycles find themselves together in racks
at places like New York City or Long Branch NJ.
They can sit idle for hours or just minutes,
and sprint through traffic or roll slowly by the sea.

Some have thin tires, others fat.
A few have baskets, occasionally a bell.
Some are black, some are white,
they are also red or yellow or pink.

But they're all just bicycles,
sharing space, co-existing on roads,
getting people to work, on errands,
helping some get exercise, have fun.

*Written and posted on 1400 Characters blog in
2013*

Doo-wop ditty

The streets were dark and quiet,
most businesses closed for the season.
But inside the doors of an Italian restaurant
just blocks from the convention center,
there was much revelry and joy.

70-somethings and other seniors
were dancing, singing, drinking, eating.
One wore a satin jacket with "Pink Lady"
written across her back.
A guy took the mike on stage
and led his friends in song.

Next day a drizzle fell,
but nothing could rain on this parade.
Doo-woppers were enjoying their annual October
weekend,
simply opening their umbrellas or ignoring the
weather
in a town that continues to make them feel young.

Old cars, old music, old people;
'57 Chevys looking as good as new,
Buddy Holly songs sounding as nice as ever.
Grandpas and grandmas were feeling as spry as
kids,

enjoying their Wildwood Days as much now as then.

Written and posted on 1400 Characters blog in 2013

Ringer

A few fast claps of the hand
after my favorite soccer team
scored a third quick goal
and off it slipped.

I looked down and saw it
catch the late afternoon
rays of the sun
as it descended
to the section of seats below
and bounce
and bounce again.

I fixed my eyes on its resting spot
and looked at the people
sitting around it, unaware.
I paused for a whole second
before quickly making my way
down to retrieve it.

I rushed past the usher
and down a few rows
to where it rested,
its gold skin still glistening,
and put it back on my finger.

"No way I'm losing my wedding ring

after 34 years with my wife
at a game where the Red Bulls
are winning,"
I explained to a curious onlooker.

And just as quickly
I returned upstairs to my seat,
to be with my wife
for the rest of the match
and, God willing,
another 34 years with my ring.

*Written and posted on 1400 Characters blog in
2015*

A Christmas card

Your sentiments can be purchased from Hallmark
for $4.99 or more,
or from another card company
for as little as 99 cents.

You can be politically correct with some people
and wish them a happy holiday,
or be forward with others
and repeat the merry Christmas mantra.

You can pay good money for the presents
on the wish lists of family and friends,
and hope the gifts you receive are those
on the list you thought hard about.

Is it the season
to pick the right cards,
say the proper greetings,
to give and get the desired gifts?

Is it that time
to make it to church,
recall fond childhood memories,
to get together with family and friends?

Is it another Christmas to celebrate
the birth of Jesus in Bethlehem,

while trying to put aside for a while
the conflict that continues around the Holy Land?

It's Christmas around the world,
that special time of the year
when Christians can celebrate the gift
that God gave to all who believe in salvation.

It can be all that,
or maybe little of it.
It's what you choose,
or what's expected from others.

Your sentiments can be purchased from Hallmark
for $4.99 or more,
or from another card company
for as little as 99 cents.

Or...

*Written and posted on 1400 Characters blog in
2015*

Voice of Amsterdam Houses:

"I was here first, Lincoln Center.
And I housed many New Yorkers
of all shapes and colors
long before all the other
tall new buildings in the 'hood.

"So, show me and my people respect
as you're entertained.
Be kind as you go to and from
cafes and restaurants,
stores and offices around town.

"It's a great big city,
and it can be a good place
for all of us, poor and rich."

*Written and posted on 1400 Characters blog in
2016*

Greenwich Village, 2016

Things are the same
and things change.
Porto Rico is still
where it's always been,
But Old El Paso
has gone Italian.

Caffe Reggio on Mcdougal
since nineteen twenty-seven
hasn't changed one bit
except for the prices,
of course.

Students walk by
in the late afternoon,
as young as ever,
perhaps as ambitious
and idealistic as ever.
Certainly, more diverse
than ever.

Today, Greenwich Village
reflects the constant
and the changes
in New York City,
perhaps the US
and our world

as well.

May it ever be so.

Written and posted on 1400 Characters blog in 2016

Abandoned

They protected New York Harbor
a century ago,
but now sit stripped
of their artillery.

In their place today grow weeds
and roam wildlife, bicyclists, casual strollers,
all warned:

"Cautious. Hazardous Area.
No unauthorized personnel
beyond this point."

"Extremely Hazardous Conditions.
Area Closed."

By Fort Hancock in Sandy Hook,
skeletons of armaments erode,
tortoise crawl across paths,
deer stand on the side of roads,
abandoned by the US Army,
left alone by summer sunbathers.

Abandoned they may feel in autumn,
abandoned again they will be in winter.

*Written and posted on 1400 Characters blog in
2016*

Homeless

The homeless man with the bushy gray beard
pushed the baby carriage
through the lot,
stopping at the sight
of a small black car.

"I ain't seen one of these
in a long time," he said.

Minutes later, the man sat down
and put tobacco into a cigarette roller.
He looked up at me,
having stepped out of the black Fiero
and now sipping a cafe con leche,
and he began to speak, clearly.

"My first car was a '70 Thunderbird."

With a startled smile, I replied,
"So was mine."

After a few minutes of conversation
about Thunderbirds, Fieros
and British sports cars,
the homeless man put his roller and cigarettes
into the baby carriage

and began to walk away.

"Have a good day," he said,
and then paused, and asked,
"Can you spare a few dollars?"

"Sure, I can spare a few dollars
for you," I replied.
Then I paused, and asked,
"Can you do me a favor?"

He looked at me.
I looked at him.

"Can you pose for a picture
with my car?" I asked.

"Sure," he replied.
"With or without my carriage?"

"It's up to you," I said.
"How ever you want to do it."

He took a moment
to comb his hair
and brush his beard
before walking over
to the Fiero.

He stood next to the black car
without his carriage,
and posed with his hand
on the roof like he owned it,
just as we did our Thunderbirds
many, many autumns ago.

Written and posted on 1400 Characters blog in 2016

The Leaf

The leaf was in the grill of a neighbor's new car.
Every time I parked, I hoped it would be gone.
But it remained, taunting me,
daring me to do something about it.
But I couldn't,
fearing I'd set off the car alarm
and have to explain myself.

Finally, I told my wife I noticed the leaf
had been stuck in the new car's grill for a week,
and it was annoying me.
She walked over to the car,
stuck her hand inside the grill,
and pulled the leaf out.
"There," she said, proudly.
"Are you happy now?"

Shortly afterwards, I was talking with another
neighbor
and mentioned the new car grill leaf story.
"Oh, you noticed it, too?" he responded.
"It was driving me crazy!"

I saw another leaf in the new car grill a few days
later.
I pulled it out, just like my wife had done, and
smiled.

No more autumn leaves in the grill of my
neighbor's new car.

Written in 2016.

After the election

Yesterday was sunny, unseasonably warm.
Outside our door, we could see surfers riding the
waves.

"We can't lose, it's election day
We can choose, it's election day
The sun is gonna rise
The stars are gonna fly"
— from Election Day, by Walter Salas-Humara and
Sam Bisbee, 2011

Today is damp, autumn-like cool.
Outside our door, we can see surfers riding the
waves.

Written and posted on 1400 Characters blog in
2016

Love the Sea, See the Love

The boy looked out at the sea
and saw a lighthouse.
Beyond its beacon he could imagine
his home, his brother, his mother.
He loved that sea dearly.
It was a direct path to everything
he longed for, for all he missed,
and love that awaited him.

The sea was also his best friend,
always there day and night,
bringing him all kinds of joy.
It refreshed him, it played with him,
at times it even fed him.

But the sea was also tempestuous,
dancing wickedly with stormy rains,
knocking against his door with anger,
once even climbing inside his room
and sweeping away some toys.
It was like the father he remembered,
all playful and attentive one day,
then angry and furious the next.

But the sea did not leave him.
It returned, calmed down

and ready to play, refresh and feed,
like the good women in his life.
And there were many good women.

His aunt, grandmother and mother
and others, all took turns
to bring him back to the sea.
They waded in its waters with him,
playing and laughing with joy
as he jumped the waves
or dove under its currents,
the silky sand under his soft feet.

But none was lovelier than the one
he married and raised their family with.
Many years she would jump right in
to share in his joy of the sea,
and see the boy who was also her man.

His eyes still sparkle by the sea,
his wife often beside him.
He likes to watch her face
as she relaxes under the sun,
the sound of the surf and children
playing around them.
When he closes his eyes,
he sees the lighthouse, feels the joy.

When he opens his eyes,

he smiles and remembers how much
he still loves the sea.
He turns to look at his wife,
and sees a love as warm as the sun.

Written and posted on 1400 Characters blog in 2017

America

Mexicans,
Russians,
Asian Indians,
Cubans,
Eastern Europeans,
Italians,
Japanese,
Chinese,
Germans,
Irish,
Africans,
British,
Native Indians.

Muslims,
Hindus,
Jews,
Catholics,
Protestants.

Black eyes,
blue eyes,
brown eyes.

Short,
tall.

And everybody else,
including you and your family,
me and mine.

"America, where are you now
Don't you care about your sons and daughters
Don't you know we need you now
We can't fight alone against the monster"
-- "Monster/Suicide/America," Steppenwolf, 1969

Written and posted on 1400 Characters blog in
2017

Subway lovers

She burrowed her weary hooded head
on his chest as the train left the station.
Across the aisle he closed his young eyes
while she cushioned his head on her chest.
A cold day in the big city didn't faze
busy Christmas shoppers and tourists.
The sounds and crowds of a packed train
didn't faze lovers underneath the hustle and bustle.

*Written and posted on 1400 Characters blog in
2017*

Family Family

Swish, swish, "What goes on out there?"
Some yelling, some tears, much heartache.

"Ah, a boy! How cute. He looks just like me."
More yelling, more tears, lots of heartache.

Disappointment. Embarrassment. Shame.

The boy goes out to sail.
The winds blow east, they blow west.
The clouds thicken, then pour rain.
He can barely stand.
The forces knock him down
and he falls in the water.
Drenched, he climbs back onboard
naked, shivering, crying.

Over and over.
Disappointment. Embarrassment. Shame.
Family.

The boy grows into a man.
He can withstand the wind.
The rain bounces off his skin.
He jumps into the water
and climbs back onto the boat.
He dries himself off slowly

and looks up at the sun,
eyes closed, heart open.

Swish, swish, "What goes on out there?"
Some lullabies, some smiles, some joy.

"Ah, a boy! How cute! He looks just like me."
More lullabies, more smiles, lots of joy.

Satisfaction. Confidence. Pride.

The man goes out to sail.
He steers his boat calmly, deftly.
Protected from a passing shower,
he resumes enjoying his time at sea.
The sunset is beautiful
and he admires the view of it.
Back ashore, he looks forward
to a restful, fulfilling evening.

Over and over.
Satisfaction. Confidence. Pride.
Family.

(Postscript:)
Mix some light tones into a dark color
and a medium shade appears.
Add brighter tones into a medium color
and a lighter hue appears.

Just like the family some people
are born into.
Just like the family some people
create for their loved ones.

Written and posted on 1400 Characters blog in
2018. Published in Fatherlands: Identities of a
Cuban American, in 2021.

The Brighton Bar, the Movie Screening

You know what to expect
but never sure what you'll get
when you walk inside the Brighton Bar.
And thus it was with the Brighton Bar movie
screening.

"If you have a black ticket, you can come inside,"
said the lady from the historical association.
"Tickets? I didn't know we needed tickets,"
responded the dozens waiting outside the screening
room.

"If you want to see the second screening, take a
green ticket,"
explained the lady from the historical association.
"Go to the Brighton Bar and have a drink while you
wait."
And around the corner walked some of the huddled
masses.

But, the Brighton Bar was closed — its staff and
patrons
had gone around the corner to see the documentary
movie.
So back out in the cold walked the huddled masses
to wait for the second screening of the movie.

"Shhhhh," beckoned the lady from the historical
association
as the huddled masses buzzed in anticipation
outside the screening room.

But they didn't need to stay quiet for long,
for a technical difficulty had delayed the first
showing.

After an hour, the patrons from the first screening
emerged
smiling, chatting, seemingly relieved at the
experience.
And in marched the green ticket holders, smiling,
chatting,
in anticipation of being entertained by the Brighton
Bar movie.

The co-host from the library welcomed the patrons
and invited them to enjoy soda and popcorn.
Then the lights dimmed, and the movie came alive
to the cheers of the second screening crowd.

The moviegoers roared as familiar faces appeared
on the screen.
They cheered as footage from years gone by
rekindled memories.
They booed when the video reminded them of
unwelcome changes
and applauded when it all ended.

They filed out with smiles across their aging faces.
Some repaired to nearby watering holes,
others simply drove home.
But one walked around the corner to the Brighton
Bar.

"Hi, I just saw the documentary and realized

I never bought one of your t-shirts," he said,
pointing to the display of items for sale behind the
bar.
"Do you have a men's size medium?"

A moment passed as the bartender spoke to the
owner.
"Actually, we're out of them and don't know
when we'll be getting some more," he told the man.
"What do you want to drink?"

The man waved him off and walked out to head
home.
You know what to expect
but never sure what you'll get
when you walk inside the Brighton Bar.

*Written and posted on 1400 Characters blog in
2018.*

Choo Choos, Parts 1-3

I.
The gentleman looked out the window,
eager to see the change in the Virginia countryside
with the Civil War over and the Union once more.

He occasionally looked down at his newspaper
to learn the latest developments in Washington
and gossip among the powerful and elite.

His wife would sometimes get his attention
and he would respond by speaking to her,
shaking or nodding his head.

All the while the choo choo kept blowing its whistle
and belching its smoke
chugging its way south,
clickety-clacking down the tracks.

II.
Nearly 100 years later, a gentleman in a suit
asked another man in a pin-striped uniform,
"What's your wife's name, and what's she like?"
The baseball player known as Choo Choo
responded,
"Her name is Mrs. Coleman — and she likes me,
Bub."

III.
The gentleman looked out the window,
staring blankly at the old Virginia towns and
landscape
after another contentious week in our United States.

He occasionally looked down at his phone
to read the latest newsfeed and tweets
and gossip among the powerful and elite.

His girlfriend would sometimes get his attention
and he would respond by speaking to her,
shaking or nodding his head.

All the while the choo choo kept blowing its whistle
and drinking its diesel
chugging its way south,
clickety-clacking down the tracks.

*Written and posted on 1400 Characters blog in
2018.*

Lonely thoughts on a beach

When I last saw you
I thought I'd be back.
I didn't think my good-bye
was so-long forever.

But here I sit on the beach,
looking beyond the cold ocean,
wondering where you are,
how you're doing,
if you still remember me.

I'm okay if you're curious.
My studies were followed by jobs
and before you know it
I was practically American.

But I'm not quite all-American.
There's no house with a white picket fence
or dogs running around a yard
or a spouse with kids in my home.

Instead there are nights on WhatsApp,
Instagram, Facebook, Twitter,
with the TV on and bed unmade.
There are weekend days on the beach,
cold days, warm days, lonely days.

Yes, I got the education and career I wanted,
but I still don't have you.
Will you be coming over any time soon?
Or should I came back for you?
Anyway, where are you?

Written and posted on 1400 Characters blog in 2019.

The Friendly City: No Vacancy

Don't try to impress me
by saying George Washington slept there.
We had seven presidents stay here
on vacation away from Washington.
Their names were Grant, Hayes, Harrison,
Garfield, Arthur, McKinley and Wilson.

These presidents put Long Branch on the map,
and the crowds from New York did come.
Soon so did others in their carriages,
four-legged and iron horses to soak up the sun,
enjoy the summer breezes, walk the bluffs and just
have fun.

Did I mention the Atlantic Ocean?
Not too many cities
can call an ocean their backyard.

Among the visitors were the wealthy
industrialists and bankers and the Bohemians.
They gambled, they drank, they ate,
and eventually most found their way home late.
But many never returned.

Others who came in their wake did decide to stay,
and formed a year-round community

that included a main street called Broadway,
complete with stores and theaters.

Long Branch got so big and diverse
with Jewish folk, African-Americans and Catholics,
even the Ku Klux Klan came to march downtown.
Fortunately, the door hit their asses on the way out.

The Mafia treated the city like a playground and
more,
playing in the Surf Lounge and paying for
the construction of the Harbour Towers high-rise.
One little pussy of a mobster bragged
on the pages of Life magazine,

"What we got in Long Branch is everything.
Police we got. Councilmen we got, too.
We're gonna make millions."

Pussy Russo was eventually found dead
with three bullets in his head
in a Long Branch spa while on furlough from
prison,
because his bosses feared he would talk too much
in order to stay and enjoy the friendly city.

We had a native son and LBHS grad
who was named poet laureate
of the entire U.S. of A.

You can read his poem "Long Branch, New Jersey,"
on a plaque in Pinsky Park on Broadway.

The pier beckoned more visitors with its
amusement rides, arcades, bars.
There were hot dogs and other kinds of matter to
put down,
which many people from across the state in fact did
as other shore towns south lured pleasure seekers
with their siren song of more, newer, better
attractions.

The city eventually became symbolized by the
Haunted Mansion,
with fake ghouls and real rats on its aging pier.
It continued creating memories for more locals
but fewer visitors before finally feeding the appetite
of a hungry fire that left behind charred splinters.

*"My city is burning down down down,
and you're not around.
You're paying attention to some other town,
you missed us burn to the ground."*

From the ashes rose the entirely new Pier Village,
with its fine restaurants, cafes, boutiques,
to attract people from all around,
but not the nostalgia of many locals, once again
proving:

CHARLES LOPEZ BRUNS

"You can please some of the people all of the time,
you can please all of the people some of the time,
but you can't please all the people all of the time."

Did Abraham Lincoln say that
while Mary Ann Todd was staying in Long Branch?
In any case, enough local citizens welcomed the
change
and re-elected Mayor Schneider six times.

Today we have Brazilians and Mexicans
and lots of other Latinos
calling the city home, with their restaurants
and various businesses on Broadway,
which still has a performing arts theater
and now even a microbrewery.

*"We've been made by these broken streets,
and now we make all these broken beats.
But we just dig it and we just dig it,
but a keep on moving on.
That's why we're fighting, that's why we're
fighting,
for where we belong."**

We still have Jewish folk a-courting
on the boardwalk Thursdays and Sundays,
and Italians and African-Americans like always.

The city even has a Sicilian-born poet laureate,
whose voice rises above the tongues of people
from all around the world on our boardwalk
and promenade every Fourth of July.

The ghosts of writers and artists past
smile at names like di Pasquale, Castaño and
Delima now.
What can they say, except
"Wow, how cool is this Long Branch?"

*"Come with the stylee if you want
to come find Long Branch rhythm.
You gotta love the way the sky looks,
when everyone lets it bring them down.
And though the sun ain't coming out,
I see light around my home town."***

The Ink Well and Brighton Bar,
home of original music,
stand alongside the Celtic Cottage
and some new Brazilian businesses,
as a synagogue is built in West End,
which isn't actually in the west end.

Did I mention the Atlantic Ocean?
Not too many cities
can call an ocean their backyard.

Long Branch is indeed a friendly city,
with no vacancy for those
who want to bring it back down
from where it rose.

*"So when these ashes turn to gold,
and when these pages start to unfold,
I have seen the best of my city,
because I've seen the worst of my city."**

—

*Copyright 2016 by David Castaño, "Burning City"
as recorded and performed by Eastbourne
**Copyright 2016 by David Castaño, "LB Stylee"
as recorded and performed by Eastbourne

*Written and posted on 1400 Characters blog in
2019.*

Morning Commuters

1. The car commuter

Start the new day with a quick coffee and bite.
Weather and traffic reports seem okay,
drive out of the neighborhood and to the highway.

From the car radio sounds "King of the Road."
The blank face smiles and then frowns,
wheels roll ever slowly and stop the commuter.

2. The train commuter

The alarm sounds, the body rolls and rises.
The day's preparations begin in a trance;
head to the station in a numb state.

A seat on the train, the voice of a conductor.
The whistle blows as the train rolls forward,
and back to sleep goes the commuter.

*Written and posted on 1400 Characters blog in
2019.*

The Queen of Corona

If me and Julio can ever find it
in the schoolyard,
we're gonna beat the crap
out of it and be on the cover of Newsweek.

Then we're going to make
a basketball out of it,
and let every good college and pro player
pound it on the floor for a whole month.

And then we're gonna turn it
to a hard rubber disk,
and give every pro hockey player
a chance to whack it with a wooden stick.

Of course we'll also shape it
into a soccer ball,
and make sure every futbol pro in the world
kicks it with all their might.

Eventually we'll reduce it to a ball with strings
wrapped tightly in cowhide,
and give every major league baseball player
a bat to hit it hard hundreds of feet.

And then we'll chisel it down even further

to a little ball with dimples,
and ask every golf tournament pro
to tee off on it with an iron club.

For good measure we'll ask thoroughbred horse
jockeys
and mighty race car engine drivers,
to run over it again and again and just leave it
behind
in a trail of muddy dirt and dust.

But we can't.
We can only avoid it like a plague
until it begins to whither and die.
And then me and Julio will find it
and kill it off once and for all.

*Written and posted on 1400 Characters blog in
2020.*

Song for Hire

Here are some words that
Need to be sung
Could use to be played
Might be helped with a tune.
So if you know a singer songwriter,
Tell them this song's for hire.

He comes to this land
With little but busy hands,
Sharp mind and desire
To have a good life.
So if you want a dreamer,
This boy's for hire.

Give me your tired your poor
The stiff lady in the harbor beckons.
They flock in by ship
And by planes and by feet
Doing work few others want.
This country's for hire.

Look at them on your screens,
Hear what they have to say.
These messages cost lots of money,
And they're all trying to appeal to you.
Figure out who might be telling truth,

SHORTS: POEMS AND SHORT STORIES

This election's winner is for hire.

He looks far and wide
For ways to make it happen.
Nothing's impossible
Or too hard, too big or too small.
So if you need to get it done,
This guy's for hire.

Writing something that makes sense
But sounds to others like nonsense.
It's fact, it's fiction, it's poetry, it's literature.
What difference does it make?
Just enjoy the sound and flow of the words,
This writer's for hire.

Freedom of speech
For all citizens rich or poor,
In various forums and media.
But that also implies the right to be wrong
And believe what you want to believe.
This truth's for hire.

Words and pictures congregate on phones and
tablets
And computers with little and big screens.
Some are offensive and others reassuring
So pick the ones you like and deny the others.
Eventually you see what you want to be believe.

This newsfeed's for hire.

The day's newspapers are delivered
To the building's varied residents.
Local papers, out-of-town papers,
Religious publications, gossip sheets.
They're all there for anyone to read.
These eyes are for hire.

I think so but I'm not sure,
Maybe possibly perhaps possibly maybe.
My gut tells me so, but my head's not sure.
It's just a sense I have somewhere,
Something in me just tells me.
This feeling's for hire.

To want and be wanted
And embrace and be cared for.
Isn't that what's it all about?
But often there's a price to pay,
Compromises and sacrifices to make.
This love's for hire.

So, there are some words that
Need to be sung
Could use to be played
Might be helped with a tune.
So if you know a singer songwriter
Tell them this song's for hire.

61

Preceding poem written and posted on 1400 Characters blog in 2020.

Seeing Clearly Now

I can see clearly now the mask has gone away
And stopped fogging up my glasses.
I can walk down the boardwalk
While breathing in the fresh air.
I can sit down with family and friends
Close enough to clearly hear what they say.

No, the coronavirus pandemic isn't quite over
But I can sense the end is near.
People are having fun together again
I know because I can see the smile on their faces.
We're resuming business as usual
As more of us return to our workplaces.

The concerts have returned to the park
And the shows are coming back to Broadway.
They're playing baseball for fans in stadiums
And new movies in the cinema theaters.
We're even able to see old cars along the beach
And read new poems in person for others to hear.

I can also see more clearly than ever the power of science
Applied by smart, hardworking and dedicated people.

I can also see more clearly now the value of
healthcare professionals,
And the importance of those we refer to as essential
workers,
Whether they have Ph.Ds or high school degrees,
Regardless of whether they are paid thousands or
hundreds each week.

I can see more clearly now why we need to hug,
And why we need to be in the presence of others.
I can see more clearly the present and the now
And the gift of life we should cherish every day,
The love we should not hold back from those dear
to us,
Or the care for one another we should willingly
provide.

I can see clearly now the mask has gone away,
The trees seem greener, the flowers prettier,
Birds are more noticeable, the sound of the ocean
louder.
People look more beautiful, simple pleasures more
precious.
Can the world be a better place for us who survived
And make us more grateful than ever to be alive?

*Written and posted on 1400 Characters blog in
2021.*

Bacalao on the Balcony

The cod was desalinated,
Cooked and seasoned to perfection,
Ready for another Christmas Eve celebration.

It was time to cool it off,
Let the flavors continue settling in the pot
So the next day it could make a splash at Grandma
and Grandpa's.

But, but, there is no room in the refrigerator.
It's already full with all kinds of other food we'll
need
For this most special of holidays and the rest of the
weekend.

There is no room in the refrigerator for the bacalao,
But it's not the first time in history needed room
was not available,
We must improvise, make do with an alternate plan
that will work well.

It's nearly freezing outside,
Why don't we just put it on our balcony
And hope none of our neighbors notice and
complain?

The bacalao is very cold in the morning,
We put it back on the stove top with a low flame,
Thinking how tasty it will be on this Christmas Eve.

Tomatoes, peppers, onions, green olives,
Potatoes, celery, sazon and cod simmering together,
In one big pot to make an amazing bacalao stew for
all to enjoy!

*Written and posted on 1400 Characters blog in
2021.*

Sea Changes

Things are not they what use to be,
It seems times are changing for the worse,
Lamented the blonde who looked too young
To be toiling 40 years at the family pharmacy
That would be closing in just a few days.

Sometimes they change for the worse,
And other times they change for the better,
Offered the sad customer who has seen many
changes
In over 60 years of living in old and
new neighborhoods,
To the very small comfort of the worker losing her
job.

The home of original music closed its doors
But hope remained the new owner would reopen it
A better place with more music, drinks, and food.
But little more than a year later it was bulldozed to
the ground,
Keeping everyone guessing what will be there next.

Maybe it will meet the same fate as the cool cafe
That was frequented at night by kids both young
and old

Who downed their Dutch coffee and grilled cheese
sandwiches.
So much in fact they tired the owner right out of
business,
Giving way to plans for more new homes and
businesses.

I see many of the changes in our neighborhood.
I sense the loss people feel around our world.
Why oh why fear change while also wanting things
better?
The sea to our east changes every day after all,
But to it we always flock to relax and recharge.

*Written and posted on 1400 Characters blog in
2023.*

Meeting Up at the Jersey Shore

I first saw you when the packed train left the
station.
I watched you with your friends during the hour we
traveled to the shore,
And pretended not to while talking to my buddies
and trying to act cool.
When the doors opened, my legs caught up to yours
and our eyes met.

I started talking to you and almost forgot about my
friends,
And your bright smile lit up your face as we chatted
with each other
Among the throng that moved quickly and loudly
toward the beach.
I whiffed the weed and saw the bottles but only
cared about you that moment.

And the moment was soon lost as chaos broke out
in the village by the sea.
There was pushing and shoving and yelling and
then fights and blood.
There was drinking and smoking and then broken
glass and debris on the street.
There was dancing and twerking on the boardwalk
and then stomping atop cars.

69

And then just like that you were apart from me, out
of sight.
I headed back to the train station and looked but
could not find you.
I searched the packed platform hoping to see you
again
And desperately moved from one car to the next on
the train home to no avail.

I remember your name but never found out where
you lived,
Or what you were doing during the rest of the
summer,
Nor what your plans were for autumn or the rest of
your life.
But I hope the two of us meet up again at the Jersey
Shore.

*Written and posted on 1400 Characters blog in
2023.*

Love and marriage and love

Before marriage there must be love,
And after marriage there must be even more love,
For love cannot be the vessel to a marriage alone.
It must also be what nurtures and grows
The happiness of the life together thereafter.

Love and marriage and love in that order,
In very good times and equally in bad,
On sunny summer days and cold winter nights,
During sounds of laughter and sniffles with tears,
When the pantry is full and glass half empty.

Love and marriage and love in that order,
Even when the jobs become very demanding,
And especially when the world becomes distracting,
Magnifying the lines between yours and mine
When they should clearly and continuously be
"ours."

Love and marriage and love in that order,
Just like this year will lead to the next,
And this decade to the one after,
As your young minds and bodies age
Evolving for better and for worse.

After marriage there must be more love,

For your everlasting love will be the foundation
That makes your strong marriage the fulfillment
Of a life you were truly destined
To share together hand in hand.

Written and posted on 1400 Characters blog in 2024.

22 Dream

The dreams by '72 were nestled in her head,
A few years after a family friend took them
For a magic carpet ride she would never forget.
"I want one, I'll have one, someday, someway," she
said.

Eighty-two gave way to '92 and the love of a man,
Along with higher education and bills and a career,
And in due time a house, two children, and minivan,
Not merely one, not just two, but eventually three.

The new millennium dawned without mayhem,
And the little boys got big and left the nest.
The jobs came and went with the passing of years,
But not those dreams of the smiling little girl.

Life at the shore with boardwalk strolls and the
beach,
Cruising along leisurely on bikes along Ocean
Avenue,
Watching the river flow and all kinds of wheels,
Spinning north, south, east, west, on the roads.

The most magical of carpet rides emerges,
Complete with the world's smallest bow tie.
"We can do this," her mate declares one spring,

And begins reaching out on their computer and
phone.

The waiting list stretches to seven months,
As the details of the dream become clearer,
Then a voice on the phone merrily announces,
"We're ready to make your dream come true."

Three months of winter later it's a reality.
Her blue eyes stare at the long body in disbelief,
The mid-engine roars, the hard roof comes down,
And she smiles while finally driving away in her 22
Dream.

*Written and posted on 1400 Characters blog in
2024.*

Happy New Year

There's not supposed to be thunder and lightning in
New Jersey
On this or any New Year's Eve or ever in
December.
Is that the Gods cursing the end of an unrighteous
year?
Or is it the latest warning that it's not nice to fool
Mother Nature?
It can't be ordinary thunder and lightning on a
winter's night.

Nothing seems that simple anymore anyhow
anyway.
Was anything ever really what it appeared?
What are those evident truths we remember?
Maybe they were only a convenience for our
minds,
A rack for our thoughts to be held safely in place.

I will be open-minded to new possibilities this year
Because everything happens for a reason,
Sometimes even for a good one or two.
Maybe the Gods are indeed all-knowing and
We mortals should just go along for the ride.

Happy New Year!

Preceding poem written and posted on 1400 Characters blog in 2025.

Newark, 9:30 p.m., Wednesday

Newark Penn Station was a grand part of New
Jersey's largest city in its day.
Now it's just an other example of the city's
struggling attempt to recover from decay.

Where's the fruit of the urban investments made in
this metropolis that once thrived?
Where are the 23 degrees The Weather Channel
claims are hovering outside?

It's a Wednesday night in Newark in the dead of
winter,
And seeing a Seton Hall basketball game at The
Rock bring some hither.
But what about many of the others inside this God
forsaken transit center?

A little girl in a pink jacket sings while sitting and
playing on the much-trodden floor.
A young woman with pink hair frowns while
strutting her black boots toward the door.

A big fellow with a black coat and white beard begs
passersby for five dollars.
A man and a woman navigate their wheelchairs
around the halls and holler.

An old guy in a hoodie sits on a wooden bench holding an iPhone and writing poetry.

Written and posted on 1400 Characters blog in 2025.

Pet Concorde

My building doesn't allow us to have dogs,
But there's nothing in the bylaws about Concordes.
Mine was gifted by my youngest son and daughter-
in-law,
And began feeling right at home after a month's
construction.

But what do you do with a regal Concorde
That's so big inside an acrylic display case?
You can't give it the run of the house day and night,
For it would surely be too easy to just trip over or
bump into.

It wouldn't make sense to take it out for walks,
Or leash it on the balcony with plants and birds.
But all the same it needs to show off and be
admired
By family and friends who come inside our modest
home.

Ah, we'll mount it to a wall.
It will be perpetually in flight,
Its webbed wings spread wide,
Wheels tucked in, nose pointing ahead.

My pride and joy supersonic jet,

2083 plastic pieces strong and fragile,
Always within view as I work in my office,
Making me smile while keeping me company.

Written and posted on 1400 Characters blog in 2025.

Status

We don't know anybody's status.
Where in the world are they from?
Did they come through the front door,
With all the necessary paperwork in order?

Are they black or yellow or red or
Just not white like our founding fathers?
How can you question who once made us great
With ambition, courage, sacrifice, and hard work?

"Give me your tired, your poor,
*Your huddled masses yearning to breathe free,**
The wretched refuse of your teeming shore.
Send these, the homeless, tempest-tossed, to me:
I lift my lamp beside the golden door."

We accepted them and we became
The greatest country in all the world.
But the times they have certainly changed
And now we want to make America great again.

So just let them return home
And curse the fate they were born with.
We don't need them to fulfill their hopes
While making this country better than ever.

We don't want people who will work hard
And reinvigorate old crumbling neighborhoods.
Why do we need more people to pick our crops,
Prepare our foods and serve and clean up after us?

What is good about having dreamers study hard
And advance science, technology, and businesses?
Why do we need low unemployment and low
inflation
Just like in the good old days we want to bring right
back?

Our country can solve all its problems
By just closing all our doors to everybody.
Oh, we can do it all alone without any foreigners,
But what is everyone's status and how did they get
here?

*Quote on the Statue of Liberty, from the Emma
Lazarus poem, "The New Colossus"

*Written and posted on 1400 Characters blog in
2025.*

The warbler and the wasp

Singing its song while flying the skies,
The warbler happily looks at the world below.
Wings flapping morning, afternoon, and evening,
She glides low before landing to find her
sustenance.

Buzzing a bit erratically above land,
The wasp darts menacingly around the area.
It manages to climb higher only when necessary,
He is seldom welcomed or greeted by anything he
sees.

But coexist the warbler and the wasp manage to do,
Just like many of God's creations on this earth of
humans.
One can sing happily while the other goes buzzing
hazardly,
Because it takes all kinds, sizes, shapes, to make
this world spin.

And so it goes night after day, all year,
Come sunshine, heat, wind, rain, cold, snow.
As youth gives way to age, business to pleasure,
War to peace, dismay to hope, short stops, and all
the way.

And then one night the warbler and the wasp meet,
Unplanned and to the detriment of all in that
moment.
The warbler was gliding low as the wasp buzzed
higher,
And both were startled and unable to avoid each
other's body.

There was no song for the warbler,
It was not sustenance to continue onward.
No buzzing for joy from the wounded wasp,
For it had encountered a mass much too large.

There was a short fall from the sky,
Straight to the cold and dark waters below.
With sounds on the way down swallowed quickly,
After a splash, some flapping, and sinking of their
bodies.

As quickly as they met unwillingly,
Their rendezvous was forever all over.
After years of singing and buzzing separately,
It all ended for them in familiar skies and waters.

Other warblers and wasps will fly,
Few will ever have such a fateful night.
Their songs and buzzing will fill the skies,
With the grace of God all over this big world.

*Preceding poem written and posted on 1400
Characters blog in 2025.*

"Thump"

We the People of the United States,
in order to form a more perfect Union,
establish justice, insure domestic tranquility,
provide for the common defence, promote the
general welfare,
and secure the blessings of liberty to ourselves and
our posterity,
do ordain and establish this Constitution for the
United States of America. *

"Thump."

I overheard loud chattering by the cyber truck in the
luxury villas,
A guy with a tough accent speaking over a
Hispanic-sounding woman.
He saw the news and was wondering how tariffs
would effect his portfolio,
She clutched the cash in her hand and was thinking
how far it would go this week.

"Thump."

The carnage was to end but actually it just began
With unprecedented and unpresidential
recklessness.

To hell with the checks and balances that model
democracy,
Just submit your cash and loyalty and be taken care
of for a while.

"Thump."

A populist who is most popular among unreality TV
fans,
Ignoring advisors to watch the tube and make policy
from there.
Brushing aside the facts and creating a distorted
reality that is fake
While scolding and belittling all those who merely
don't see it his way.

"Thump."

Many Americans are part of the same grand old
party,
One that once championed freedoms in lands where
little existed.
Now they're watching the leader of the free world
rub shoulders with tyrants,
Bathing in flattery and accepting their gifts and just
letting bygones be bygones.

"Thump."

Oooh oooh that funny smell,
Can't you whiff that terrible odor?
Hey, what exactly is that awful sound?
Everybody just take a look at what's going down.

"Thump."

It's this great country of ours free falling
In the little hands of a delusional uncrowned king
Who wears a suit and tie rather than flowing robes
And tramples on the Constitution he was elected to
protect.

"Thump."

*the Preamble to the US Constitution, written in
1787

Written in 2025.

The first time

He couldn't wait for that Saturday
When the family planned to go to the stadium
And see a baseball game for the very first time.

The ball players on the field were in color
Just like in the young boy's cards at home,
Unlike what he saw on his family's television.

The sun warmed him and thousands of others
When he settled inside the major league ballpark
And saw his uniformed heroes hit, run, field, throw.

Oh they did look so far away below him
But the grass they played on was so green
And the people in the stands so many and loud.

The rookie hit a homer over the right field fence
And the veteran pitcher threw six strong innings,
But the game was tied entering the bottom of the
ninth.

Young fans like him held on to their free Louisville
Sluggers
And banged them on the ground to cheer for the
home team
While men in the stands sipped their last beers of
the afternoon.

89

One batter reached base, then a second,
And soon the sun looked down on a swirl of dust
That surrounded the three men around home plate.

"Safe!" said the man in black
As he spread his arms horizontally
And the throng of thousands cheered excitedly.

On the crowded train home the boy smiled
With his brother and uncle seated with him
Replaying what he just saw inside his capped head.

Written in 2025.

Shorts

There I stood at all of five years
Celebrating my cousin's birthday
With annoyance on my face as a
Silly small pointy hat sat on my head,
Not because of the shorts pulled up and
Over my waist revealing the cuts and bruises
A boy can accumulate on his very active legs.

I liked shorts when I was a child,
Wearing them in various colors
with and sans belts or suspenders
For all kinds of occasions,
Even my very own baptism
And other times much more fun.
Wearing shorts meant good times!

But not so much as a teenager,
When shorts were kinda uncool
Unless they were cut off blue jeans
That wore out and faded and frayed.
Then it was nearly almost sort of hip,
Although hot pants and short shorts
Were worn stylishly by leggy pretty girls.

Larry the Celtic wasn't flattered by his,
Though it hardly effected his shooting.
But certainly many soccer players were,
Perhaps raising the popularity of the sport,

And in due time helping make shorts cool again
So that more people began wearing them all the
time,
Even in freezing temperatures and with snow on the
ground.

Now I'm all grown up and don them often
When I'm out walking or just hanging around,
Visiting family and friends with a pair of them
And trying to keep them crisp as they hold my keys
And wallet and phone and whatever else I have with
me.
I can even work with them because nobody on a
Teams call
Has any idea what's below my shirt as we sit and
talk business.

I posed in a backyard with cargoes this summer
Trying to recreate the photo of my five-year-old self
In order to use them on the back cover of a new
paperback
That contains a collection of nearly all my poems
and short stories,
Many no doubt composed as I sat comfortably with
calves exposed
Searching for the right words to express a particular
thought or feeling
On complex topics or in some cases about subjects
as simple as … shorts.

Written in 2025.

<u>Guest poem:</u>

Ballad of the 59th Street Subway Station

by Lou Bruns

Deep to the bowels where the smells and stench
reek,
go the strong men and women, the fools and the
meek.
But the scene here unfolds, like a madman's
nightmare,
and if you are sane you'll just stay away from there.

The stage is New York, and the actors are men,
with strong supporting roles from the dead and the
damned.
The setting's all perfect...a bum's at the door,
and then from a distance, you hear a dull roar.

The station is cleared for the coming onslaught,
the transit cop waits, his nerves tied in knots.
And then from the earth comes the five o'clock
train,
rolling and rocking like an old drunken lame.

Hundreds and thousands (and then maybe more),
were squashed in that train, right up to the door.

The train grinds its wheels to force itself halt,
and then from the cars came a flash and a bolt.

Hundreds and thousands crammed fighting for
space,
it mattered not who you were or what was your
race.
And then from the lungs came a cry of despair,
it seems that another train had pulled up in there.

Fat ladies and models; yes even the meek,
the hippies, the hardhats, the cops and the freaks.
They all pushed and shoved to get down the hall,
and out through the gates where the smog greets
them all.

For some odd ten minutes, this scene here went by,
and all that I've written is not just a lie.
The screams of the infants, whose mom's breast
they wish,
the odor of armpits that smelled like old fish.

Then suddenly, as if God himself heard our call,
the station went quiet; you could hear a pin fall.
And the wino; whose eyes have just witnessed this
scene,
swore off of the bottle, to prevent more DTs.

CHARLES LOPEZ BRUNS

*Preceding poem written by Lou Bruns in 1972 and
posted on 1400 Characters blog in 2016*

<u>Short stories by Charles Lopez Bruns</u>

More Than Street Wise

As the dirty subway pulled out of the elevated station, leaving behind it the flashing lights and piercing noises of Coney Island, the two boys slumped down on the first empty seats they saw and looked at each other with sighs of relief. Eric, a tall and thin sleepy-eyed black, wiped the sweat from his brows and leaned his head against the back of the ripped seat. Eduardo, a little heavier and slightly shorter, ran his fidgety fingers through his brown hair and stared at the map across the aisle. Yes, he silently confirmed to himself, they had gotten on the right train after all. Eric, staring at the huge fans on the ceiling, opened his mouth as if to say something, but soon closed it and shut his eyes.

"Hey, Eric," Eduardo blurted as he leaned over and tugged at his friend's well-worn polo shirt, "keep your eyes open. Maybe they got on the train. We gotta watch out!"

Eric, dismayed by his buddy's advice, straightened up his exhausted body and took a long look at the rest of the passengers on the half full train. "We don't have a thing to worry about now," he replied. They have to be crazy to try anything here."

"That's just it, " Eduardo quickly shot back, "they're crazy! You saw what they tried to do back there."

Trying to ignore his friend's words but obviously failing, Eric nodded and said, "Okay, okay. We'll be careful."

The subway slipped away from the dark blue sky and dim Brooklyn streetlights and into a blackened underground tunnel. DeKalb ... Boro Hall ... Delancey ... West 4th Street ... the same stations the two boys had passed by dozens of times before suddenly became more than just dull marble and steel configurations. Now the boys became more aware of which stations were better lit than others and which of them had more exits than others.

Eventually, the muffled voice on the P.A. announced that the next stop was 59th Street. The boys, almost instinctively, rose from their seats slowly and started moving towards the door. As they emerged out of the train and towards the steps leading up to the street, Eduardo stopped, grabbed Eric's arm, and shouted, "Look, there they are! Oh no, he just saw us! Run!"

Eric paused a minute to confirm Eduardo's observation with his own eyes, then quickly turned around and started running. His long strides were soon catching up to Eduardo's quick, short steps, and he yelled loud enough to cause two old fat ladies with heavy shopping bags to turn around and pay notice, "Are they still coming? Take a look!

Eduardo, beginning to run out of breath, glanced quickly over his shoulder and shouted, "Yea! Come on, we gotta keep moving! We'll try to lose them when we get outside!"

The two boyish figures shot out from the subway station and into the dusk all in one stride. They were immediately followed by two taller figures. The frenzied chase continued up the dark street where the school Eric and Eduardo would be returning to in a few weeks was located. As they chugged past an aged Catholic church, Eric looked back to see how far back their pursuers were. To his surprise and relief, he no longer saw them. Instead, all he could see were a few old men walking and some cars whizzing by on the adjacent avenue. "Hey, stop," he beckoned to his friend, "I don't see them. Maybe they turned up the other street."

The boys stopped their frantic pace and sat down in front of the old school building. They stared across the street, where bulldozers sat quietly and mountains of dirt stuck out above a wooden fence which had colorful graffiti scrawled across it. Across the lot they could see the gymnasium of a local high school. Again, scenes which they usually just took for granted now looked so interesting, so fascinating. Home sweet home? It was close enough. After all, the huge apartment complex was the only place the boys had ever lived in.

They continued walking home, stopping only to see the televisions on display at a storefront. They fixed their eyes for a few minutes on a show in progress.

"C'mon, Eduardo," Eric said during the first commercial break. "I've seen that one about 15 times."

"Yea, me too," Eduardo remarked with a shrug. " I'm just waiting for the day he gets chased around town."

"Ha," Eric replied, "That would be something."

"You gonna stop by for a while?' Eduardo asked his buddy as he neared his apartment building.

"Yea, just a little while," Eric replied, "I wanna see that new bat your ma got you before someone steals it." The two entered the door leading to the hallway when, suddenly, a voice from behind alarmed them.

"Well, you two little peckers, just keep walking straight ahead to the staircase. Don't run or do anything else stupid." The voices behind their backs suddenly became large hands across the back of their necks. As they entered the staircase, their tormentors twirled them around and confronted them face-to-face, or, rather, fist-to-face.

"What did we do, man?' Eduardo said, nervous and stunned, "what's going on?'

"Shut up, punk," one of the assailants remarked. "Now listen! I was just having a nice time minding my own business down at Coney Island when I saw you two, and it just ruined my day! My little brother's been complaining about you two picking on him. I recognized your faces from a class picture he showed me the other day. Now we gonna have to take care of you because you know we just have to watch out for the little brother."

A barrage of fists landed on Eduardo's and Eric's faces. They moaned, jelled, and fell to the ground as the thugs gave them each a kick in the face before hastily departing.

Blood flowed freely from Eric's mouth, while Eduardo's face was dominated by the cuts near his eyes.

Down the steps pranced a diminutive figure. Shocked at what he saw, he drew closer to the two wallowing bodies but drew back quickly when he recognized them. "Suarez and Wilson!"

"Yea, that's us," Eric responded.

"What happened, guys?' the undersized boy asked.

"Got mugged," Eric replied while Eduardo started picking himself up. "Don't just stand there, you little faggot. Help us or get the hell out."

"No," the boy replied, "help yourself. I ain't no faggot. I'm gonna tell my big brother."

"Oh my God, Eric," Eduardo said, "he's got a big brother too! Come on, let's get the elevator to my place." The two staggered over to the elevator outside the staircase.

Their wounded faces mirrored greater agony seconds later when two tall and one short familiar figures entered the hallway. Eduardo turned quickly to run, but Eric grabbed him and looked at him dejectedly as if to say, "what's the use?"

"Well, well, well," one of the assailants said with a wide grin, "it looks like you boys didn't learn your lesson. I didn't even make it across the street before my little brother here came running to me complaining about these two bleeding guys calling him a faggot. Just what do I have to do to get you creeps off his case?"

The two big boys started shoving Eric and Eduardo through the door leading to the staircase when, suddenly, two husky figures emerged from the elevator. The two thugs muzzled their victims in an attempt to hide what was happening, but it was to no avail. One of the boys stepping out of the elevator, Manuel, a rough-looking, dark complexioned 13-year-old, leaned his head over towards the staircase and spotted the affair.

"Hey, what's going on?' the beady-eyed Puerto Rican demanded to know, "you beating up those little guys?"

When he moved closer to the two taller boys, he recognized Eduardo, and a look of bewilderment entered his round face. "Suarez, what are they doing to you?"

Eduardo started to open his mouth when he felt the blade of a knife poke his back slowly. He stood quietly, saying nothing. Eric, seeing through the corner of his eye why his friend was speechless, struggled to free himself from his captor, but was unsuccessful. Momentary silence set in. Manuel and his friend, Celerino, stared at Eduardo and Eric and the two lanky black boys holding them. They, in turn, returned the scowls. Two young girls with jump ropes entered the building and pressed the button for the elevator, but no one looked.

"Let them go, Jones," Manuel commanded. Nobody moved. Only the sound of a passing bus could be heard.

"I said let 'em go," Manuel, his voice rising slowly, repeated. Again, silence set in. Nothing moved ... nothing but Celerino's hands, which entered his pocket and exited with a sharp six-inch knife.

Manuel stuck his arm out as if to tell his friend that a knife wouldn't be necessary to win this confrontation, but Eric blurted out, "he's got -- " before his tormentor muzzled him more forcefully. Again, more silence.

"You let them go or we cut your chocolate hands off, Jones," Manuel warned. The elevator door suddenly swung open and a feeble man with gray hair and a cane followed a middle-aged woman out into the hall. She screamed when she saw the seven boys ready to erupt into violence, and the old man with the black outfit turned slowly and shook his head. Manuel and Celerino dropped their heads, and the two tall boys by the door let go of Eduardo and Eric. More silence.

"Hi Father," Manuel uttered. The old man walked slowly towards the boys and stopped to look at each of them in the eye.

"Eduardo and Eric, go home. Michael, you too," he said, still staring at the four older boys. "Put them away," he commanded in a low but stern voice. They did. "I don't know what it is you people are ready to kill each other over, and I don't particularly care. There is nothing in this world of ours that justifies young kids knifing each other to death."

Eduardo, stepping out of the elevator on the 10th floor, hurried to the door leading to his apartment. He entered to see his younger brother, Luis, sitting on the floor watching television. His mother, shocked at the fresh scars on his face, looked at him angrily and shouted, "*Adonde tu estaba, muchacho*!"

"*Na ma fuy a la casa de Eric, mama*," he replied meekly.

"*No, no! Yo lo llame y tu no estaba aye*!'" She walked swiftly at him, and he shielded his head while his mother lectured him on the virtues of honesty and asked him where he had gotten his scars.

Eric, walking down the street quickly towards his apartment, tried to think of what he would tell his mother. When he finally arrived home, he found only his little sister there, intently watching television. you. "Eric, where have been all day?' she asked.

"Nowhere, why?" he replied .

"Just curious," she answered.

"Hey, Chip, wasn't that neat," the voice on the television screen said. "Yea, Robbie, it was a lot of fun. It's always fun to go to the fun fair with Dad. It's the only time all year we get to eat cotton candy!" A shiny new car flashed by the screen, stopping by an old farm which had hand-painted signs advertising apples, tomatoes and corn for sale. "You boys want to stop and pick up some goodies?' another voice asked. "Oh, yea, Dad, let's pick up some corn."

Eric, slumped on a sofa, closed his eyes. He opened them again for a few seconds when an advertisement came on the screen, but he slowly shut them again when the show came back on.

Eduardo, sitting on a chair in the corner of his living room, held his head in his hands and looked blankly to the screen.

Within minutes, tears. filled their eyes and trickled down their cheeks.

Written in 1978.

A Woman and Man

She studied his eyes carefully, looking for them to confirm or deny the words which were flowing freely from his mouth. He paused, met her inquisitive eyes with his own, and, in a tone of genuine concern, spoke again.

"Do you understand what I'm saying?"

"Yes, I do," she answered. "I do, really. A lot of what you say is true. But I'm not sure yet that it's such a positive thing. There certainly are a great number of people who feel the way you do, but I think a lot of them remain unhappy."

"Yes, that may be true," he nodded, "but it's early yet. The real test will come in ten or fifteen years, when their lives will have more or less fallen into some type of pattern. I think that they will handle their middle- age years better as a result of their self-fulfilling experiences while young."

"That's what I'm not so sure about," she interjected. "After years of being so concerned about just themselves, how can they develop a concern for a family and the rest of the world. They'll be spoiled by self-indulgence!"

"I don't think so. Quite the contrary, they will almost be bored by it. They will have saturated their freedoms. They will be so self-fulfilled that they will actively search to share this happiness with others. And, after all, isn't that the ultimate human goal?"

She shook her head slowly. Even though she didn't fully agree with the point he was making, she respected the logic he used to support his beliefs. It was always refreshing for her to see a man look beyond the mere surface of his reality. For this reason, she continued to focus her eyes on his. Surely his eyes would reveal the true depth of his words.

He was aware in his own mind of her curiosity, but he wasn't sure just how to confront it. So, he postponed doing so. He looked at her in a moment of silence but was careful not to let his eyes expose his soul.

"Do you want to hear some music?" she asked. "I've got a pretty good collection."

"Okay," he answered. "How about some old Kinks? Do you have any of their albums?"

"No," she replied with some degree of disappointment. "I have a lot of Dylan, though. You're into his music, aren't you?"

"Sure. Dylan would be just fine."

She rose to put a record on the stereo. He observed her soft steps and delicate manners and slipped into the adjoining kitchen to pour them more wine.

"This is pretty good wine, isn't it?" he asked as he walked back into the parlor.

"Yes, it is," she said. "I usually prefer semi-dry red wines, but this is just fine. I mean, I already feel it."

She grinned with those words, and he smiled back to her. Suddenly, each was at a loss for words. She looked for him to renew their conversation, but he sat back on the sofa and concentrated on the wine and music. He hardly seemed aware that she was staring at him. Finally, she penetrated the silence with an awkward question.

"How personal is Dylan's music to you?"

He knitted his brows in puzzlement. He groped for an answer but was unsuccessful. "I'm not quite sure what you're asking."

"Hmm. Well, what I'm asking is, how much of his music can you identify with personally? Can you relate to it with your own life experiences?"

"I can relate to a lot of his love songs," he answered. "The way he portrays women and men-women relationships in general are very real to me. His protest stuff I'm not too sure of, though."

"That's interesting," she said, curiously. "I don't think he comes across too positively about women in his songs. In fact, I would say he's generally pretty negative about them. He's had some positive songs on the subject, but his better ones are full of frustration and desperation, don't you think? Can you really relate to that?"

He took a long look at her, unsure of just how to respond to such a question. Although he would not show it, he was quite impressed by the manner she dared him to expose his feelings on such a personal matter. He wasn't used to having a woman challenge him on such a level.

She sensed his immediate futility. And, with a touch of shame, she was proud. It was merely an objective question on the surface. But she knew he would have to search beyond the surface for an answer. He knew that she realized this.

"Yes, I guess I can," he said, slowly. He took another sip of wine and pondered an explanation. "I don't think most relationships between men and women are happy and fulfilling ones. Quite the opposite. I think real needs and wants are usually left unfulfilled, even among people who spend a lifetime together and claim to be content. I think Dylan senses this. Do you?'

She wasn't quite ready to handle the question herself, so she took another sip of wine and delayed giving an answer. He had given a simple but smart reply and now was challenging her. She was used to having men pose two-sided questions to her, but not in the same manner he did. This made her even more curious and caused her to continue staring into his eyes. She just knew they would betray him eventually!

"Yes, I do," finally was her reply. But she spoke no more.

He felt that she was somewhat confused by the direction their conversation was heading. He got up to pour some more wine in the hope that the subject would be dropped. He sensed a victory in this mind game of theirs but didn't see a need to play it out. Apparently, however, she had different thoughts.

"I'm not so sure women are the reason for all the unfulfilling relationships," was her comeback. "I think Dylan implies this with all his negativeness-"

"I don't," he shot back.

"Maybe not," she remarked. "You probably just assume it."

"I don't assume anything," he said, hastily. "Anyway, we're talking about Dylan, aren't we?"

"Yes. But you say you can relate to him," she remarked. She continued staring at him in the hope that, finally, bis eyes would reveal something his words didn't. But they did not.

As the evening wore on, their conversation became less intense and more informal. Once they ceased to probe each other's personal feelings, the atmosphere loosened. Still, because an initial contact with each other's emotions had been so interesting, curiosity continued to rest in them. Finally, after the wine and conversation began to wane, he started to tire.

"Well, I guess I'll be making my way home," he said. His eyes focused on her. She stared at him, waiting for him to say more. He approached her slowly and kissed her softly on the forehead. He then backed up a step and they stood looking deeply into each other's eyes. She continued her search and within a few moments she could sense a trace of helplessness and frustration in his eyes reach out feebly to her. A compassionate glow entered her own eyes and spread to the rest of her face. Suddenly, he felt totally defenseless, totally exposed.

"You can stay with me if you want," she said, softly.

"Do you want me to?" he asked .

"Yes."

They embraced and she realized he was just a man, she just a woman. And she was so glad.

Written in 1978.

Sir James and Freddie

In an old, dimly lit restaurant, Sir James growled as he sipped the last drops from a glass of beer. His afternoon had been uneventful, and he was resigned to his dinner being the same. He alternated between staring at the long black limousines and the cool weather which awaited him outside, and the rude waiters which seemed to have forgotten him inside.

"Hey, waiter, where's my food?" he asked as one hurriedly passed him.

"It'll be coming, just be patient," was the answer he received. He raised his empty glass, but the waiter was gone before he could ask for another beer.

Instead, he growled some more.

He sat dejectedly for 15 more minutes before his dinner finally arrived. Then, it took another few minutes for him to decide that he really wanted to put it in his stomach. It was an odd shaped and colored dinner entree he had ordered. He quickly concluded that he erred in his selection, but he also realized he didn't have the time or patience to order something else. So, he just sat and ate it with a long face.

A few miles away, in a well-lit and modernly furnished office, Freddie laughed and smiled as he talked on the telephone. He woke up in the morning sensing it was going to be a special day, and he was concluding his afternoon's work with the realization that he was right. After hanging up the telephone, he put on his jacket, waved goodbye to his secretary, and caught the elevator downstairs.

He grabbed one of his favorite foods, a hot dog with mustard, sauerkraut, and red onions, from a street vendor a block away, and chewed on it as he continued making his way towards the subway. With his spirits so high, he found it thrilling just to look up and observe the menagerie of lights which were popping out of the tall buildings and darkening sky.

Nowhere were the lights brighter than at the bullfighting arena in the middle of town. There, a crowd began to assemble for the night's major attraction -- a football game between the local pro team and a club from London. It was the most talked about sporting event in the area in many months.

Freddie was typical. He had purchased his ticket weeks in advance of the game and made sure that no plans would keep him away from the city on this night. On the subway train he met several other gentlemen heading towards the arena.

"It should be a splendid game, don't you think, mate?" he asked one fellow passenger. "Let's hope so," the man replied. "If it isn't, I'll be quite disappointed. I do hope the Brits are up for it." The excited chatter of the passengers almost, for once, rivaled the music floating through the train's speakers.

Sir James moved along slowly towards the arts and theater center in a limousine. Restless, he listened to the din of the traffic outside his window. He grunted as pedestrians passed him by. Occasionally, when they tapped on the hood or spat on the fender, he growled. The driver ignored him.

After what seemed like eternity, the dirty limousine pulled up to the side of the theater. Sir James handed the driver some loose change and limped outside. He growled again when the large clock across the street revealed that he was 10 minutes late for the opening. After purchasing his ticket for the opera, he found his seat in the half empty theater. Within half an hour, he was snoring.

"Hey, man," a voice behind him prodded. "Keep your noise to yourself. If you wanna sleep, find yourself a corner in the art museum."

"Aw, shut up." Sir James replied. "Leave if you don't like it. My dollar smells the same as yours." After taking a quick look at the number of other grubby men who were sleeping, he squirmed in his seat and closed his eyes.

As the subway pulled up to the crowded station in the middle of town, Freddie and his fellow sportsmen rose from the comfort of their seats and edged towards the door. They exited in a quick pace, continuing their conversation on the night's game as they walked up to street level.

The entourage continued their pilgrimage towards the arena located just a few blocks away from the station. The closer they drew, the more crowded the streets and sidewalk became. The excited chatter of fans grew deafening as Freddie approached the gate, his cherished ticket in hand.

He found his seat in time to watch the London club casually warming up on the dirt pitch below. He exchanged greetings with the group of fans surrounding him and quickly began alternating between rubbing his hands and yelling at the visiting stars.

"Do you think they'll start three forwards?" a well-dressed spectator to his left inquired.

"Oh, I imagine they will," Freddie replied. "It's only an exhibition match. They'll probably give their new Dane a chance. I think that's him over there."

Sir James was rudely awakened from his nap at the theater when an usher banged a flashlight on his shoulder. He opened his eyes and noticed that an old dirty curtain was drawn down on the stage.

"Hey, you, it's intermission," the usher snapped. "Go to the bathroom now so you won't have to piss on our chair later."

The usher waited a few moments for Sir James to rise from his chair and walk towards the lobby. Once there, he found his way to the men's room. He grubbed a cigarette and a few swigs of vodka during his ten minutes inside but didn't urinate. A theater employee eventually came in and ordered everyone back to their seats for the conclusion of the evening's opera performance.

The crowd inside the arena let out a huge roar as the local club scored the match's first goal with just moments remaining in the first half. Confetti showered on the players as they hugged each other in celebration.

"What a wonderful goal that was," Freddie said to a neighboring spectator minutes later as they both rose to buy some refreshments. The game was turning out to be as exciting as all the fans had hoped. The London club was entertaining everyone with their skill, but the locals were in top form.

The spectators were busy talking and laughing with excitement during the intermission. They hurried back to their seats as the teams filed out for the start of the second half. Chants of encouragement for the local team started up as soon as the referee blew the whistle to restart play.

"You can't sing, fat lady!" Sir James blurted out. "You're awful. Where'd they find you?" Ripples of grumbling and booing spread through the theater slowly. Some of it was directed at Sir James, some at the performer on stage.

The woman ignored the audience and kept on singing. An empty liquor bottle hurled on stage landed a few yards away from her, but she paid it no mind. When some fruit hit Sir James in the head, however, she paused momentarily to smile.

The ushers hurried down the aisles and began escorting some of the men outside of the theater. Sir James offered no resistance when they grabbed his arms and dragged him out to the street. He merely growled. After picking himself up off the ground and kicking the door, he pulled down his zipper and urinated on the building.

With the score even at 1-1 and the match drawing to a close, the fans in the arena rallied vociferously behind the local club. What happened in the final minutes, however, was unprecedented and entirely unexpected.

A player shot the ball so hard, that it shattered one of the wooden walls just to the side of the goal. Several bulls escaped from their stalls underneath the stands and stampeded towards the red-shirted London players. The fans cheered wildly at the spectacle. They laughed as the athletes fled from the charging bulls by scrambling around the dirt pitch and climbing the walls onto the stands.

"Unbelievable!" Freddie exclaimed. "Look at that guy down there. The bull's stomping all over him! He's getting gored. He's bleeding! We're really getting our money's worth - - a special football game and a preview of tomorrow night's program!"

His evening at the opera ended, Sir James flagged an awaiting limousine. He directed the driver towards a restaurant in the lower end of town, where he hoped to salvage his day with a decent dessert and coffee.

It was well into the night now, and Sir James locked his door as a precaution against thieves. He stared out the window and growled as the driver tried fruitlessly to avoid the graffiti artists and negotiate the vehicle out of yet another traffic jam.

In the subway after the match, Freddie and a group of other sportsmen excitedly recounted the evening's happenings. They all agreed that the local club had played exceptionally well and speculated on how badly some London players might have been injured by the charging bulls.

"I think it'll be quite some time before the Londoners come back to the city," Freddie predicted. "It must've seemed like they were up against 22 opponents -- 11 football players and 11 bulls!"

They laughed at the comment as the subway stopped, and doors opened. Freddie smiled and waved as he made his way through the station and up the stairs. Once on the sidewalk, he began walking towards the fast-food restaurant across the street. He often ended special evenings with a tasty hamburger and French fries.

Suddenly, he noticed some frantic activity inside a parked limousine. He rushed over and banged his hands on the windshield.

"Police! Police!" he yelled aloud to everyone in general. Two knife-wielding youths bolted from the limousine when they heard Freddie. They dashed away and were quickly given chase by a pair of foot patrolmen. Freddie leaned into the limousine and found the driver bloodied and apparently unconscious. He also heard Sir James growl in the back seat.

"They didn't get a dime from me," he said, vengefully. "The driver must be stupid. He left both front doors unlocked. He should've known better."

Sir James limped out of the limousine as Freddie attempted to revive the driver. He began walking away from the small crowd that was milling around the scene, but Freddie grabbed his shoulder and stopped him in his tracks.

"Aren't you going to at least wait and explain to the police what happened?" he asked.

"Nah, what for?" Sir James replied. "It won't make a difference. They don't really care about everyday limo muggings. They've got too many other problems to worry about."

Freddie hesitated for a moment, then offered to buy Sir James a burger and fries. Sir James gladly accepted the rare opportunity to eat some decent food. Shortly after the two sat down with their orders, the police arrived and pulled the driver out of the limousine. Freddie and Sir James looked out the window and munched on their snacks as an ambulance took the wounded driver away.

"The city really should do more about crime," Freddie remarked. Sir James was still too busy biting into his hamburger to reply.

"I realize it's not safe out there for the average person," Freddie continued.

"Oh, you do?" Sir James said, ketchup dripping from his mouth. "You ride in subways and eat good food at fast joints like this. What do you really know about the average person? I ate garbage at some restaurant and got stuck in a lousy opera tonight. What did you do, go to the arena for the big game?"

"Hey, I understand," Freddie said, almost apologetically. "But all of us have to live together in this city. We're all human beings, and we all have our problems."

"Yeah, buddy," Sir James shot back. " But some of us have a lot more problems than others. That's pretty obvious when you look around."

"No, that's not true," Freddie replied. "Is anybody really better off than anybody else these days? I don't think so. It may just seem that way on the surface."

123

Sir James growled, burped, and limped out of the restaurant and into the night. Freddie buttoned his jacket and whisked off into the same night.

Written in 1986.

Home

The bus rolled off the New Jersey Turnpike and onto another highway. The boy looked out the window and recognized the New York City skyline in front of him. So did many of the other kids on the bus. Suddenly, it was noisier than it had been at any time since they boarded the yellow bus a few hours earlier in a place called Pennsylvania. There this morning, many of them saw each other for the first time in two weeks, since a similar bus had dropped them off in a town that was nothing like the city they lived in. It had been a surprisingly quiet bus ride for the group of boys and girls who ranged in age from eight to twelve, but seeing the Empire State Building and other tall buildings excited them.

Even Luis smiled at the sight. He enjoyed his time with a family that had welcomed him into their house the past two weeks. He did not particularly care for the food they had to eat, but he got along fine with the boy who lived in the house. He enjoyed playing on the grass in their back yard, and also liked it when other kids in the neighborhood came over. Nearly all of them were nice to him, asking if he wanted to play games, some of which he was not familiar with. A few of the boys, however, were not so kind. One of the older boys made fun of the shape of his head, calling Luis "football head." He had heard that before, in school, and tried to ignore the comment. Another boy asked him what kind of name "Suarez" was.

"Are you Puerto Rican?" this other older boy asked.

"Yes, I am," Luis replied with a slight accent they were not familiar with. "Are you?"

"No!" the boy said. "I'm Slovak."

"You're what?" Luis asked. "What's that?"

"I'm Slovak," the boy said again. "I don't know what that is, but it's what my parents say."

Some of boys overhearing the conversation laughed, and continued running around with a couple of big balls they threw at other friends when they weren't looking. These were the same kids who got together the day before in someone else's back yard to go in a pool. Luis did not bring a bathing suit with him, but the boy's mother was nice enough to let him wear one of her son's. Luis was never in an above-ground swimming pool before, and he enjoyed being in the water with the other boys even though he stood on his toes and stayed near the ladder, clinging to the side.

Most of the time, however, Luis stayed in the house and yard of the family that was hosting him. He and the only child who lived there, Joseph, had just finished second grade and were trying to enjoy the summer before going back to their schools, which were a couple of states and a few hundred miles apart. Luis noticed Joseph spoke with a slight stutter, and listened closely when he talked to make sure he understood his words. This wasn't difficult when the two of them were together outside without a television or radio to distract their attention. And since it was so hot most days, they didn't want to stay inside, where there was no breeze.

The few dozen kids on the bus were returning home, in most cases, after a couple weeks with different families in "the country," courtesy of something they heard grown-ups call the Fresh Air Fund. Luis recognized a few of the kids from the playground in his neighborhood, but he did not know most of them. The relative silence on the bus until that point was probably because most of the kids also did not know many others. They had all just said good-bye to the families and new friends they spent two weeks with, and some realized they would probably never see these people again. Luis had some of those bittersweet feelings until he recognized a few of the tall buildings in the distance. They were some of the same ones he would often stare at from the window of his bedroom in the tenth-floor apartment he shared with his mother.

Two weeks earlier, before they got on the subway train that took them to the midtown Manhattan street where he would board the bus that transported him to Pennsylvania, Luis watched his mother pack a few underwear, socks, t-shirts and shorts into a big paper bag. She told him to make sure everything came back home with him, and he nodded his head.

Before he said good-bye to Joseph and his parents for the bus ride home, Luis checked to make sure all his clothes were packed in the bag. He squeezed in a couple of new shirts and a pair of pants the host family gave him, which caused a small rip near the handle of the bag. He carried it carefully to the bus stop where the other kids and a bunch of grown-ups waited for the bus back to the city.

As the bus made its way through the Lincoln Tunnel, a couple of the kids shrieked with excitement. For the first time that day, the bus driver yelled for everybody to calm down. His admonishment worked for less than a minute. When the bus exited the tunnel and rolled into the city, the kids made a lot more noise. Some were jumping up and down by their seats, pointing at the window toward the interesting sights outside. Finally, after a few minutes, the bus arrived at the same spot where it had picked up the kids two weeks earlier.

The scene made Luis think back for a moment what it was like when the bus had dropped everybody off in Pennsylvania. The kids were excited then, but it was more of a muted joy. No one knew who to look for – only a tag with their name and that of the host family identified them – but they were sure someone would walk up to them, introduce themselves, and welcome them to come to their home for their vacation. At that point, they would ride in a car, sometimes with the child or two they would be playing with for the next couple of weeks, and answer a bunch of questions about the bus ride and, perhaps, themselves.

Luis had told Joseph and his mother that the bus ride was long, pretty quiet, but interesting. He explained that he saw lots of cars and trucks on the highway, and farm after farm and some tractors and other kinds of vehicles he never saw before off the side of the road as they got closer to the end of the ride. The mom, who looked about the same age as his mother and wore sunglasses, said there were indeed lots of farms around.

"I'm sure you don't see many of them around New York!" she said, smiling.

"No, I don't," Luis smiled back, looking over at Joseph seated next to his mom in front of the car. "Have you ever been to New York?"

"Oh dear, it's been years," she responded. "Maybe ten years. I don't think Joseph has ever been there. You were in Philadelphia to see a baseball game with your dad, though, weren't you, Joseph?"

"Yes, just last year," Joseph replied. "We saw the Phillies beat the Mets at Connie Mack Stadium."

Luis had not yet been to a major league baseball game in New York. He would occasionally notice a game was on television while he was turning the stations to find a favorite cartoon to watch, but he wasn't very interested in them. Some of his classmates would get excited about the baseball cards they held in their hands, and Luis would overhear them mention names like Mickey Mantle, Willie Mays, and Casey Stengel. He thinks he saw Casey Stengel on television once, and he looked like a very old man.

When the driver parked the bus on the busy Manhattan street and shut off the motor, the kids were jumping and noisy. Some of them started waving frantically at people they recognized.

"Mommy, mommy! *Aqui, aqui*!" one, then two and three, yelled.

"Hello pop!" another voice cried out.

Luis felt overwhelmed by all the excitement on the bus. He was also quite taken by all the people who were crowded on the sidewalk with their eyes fixed on the windows of the bus. He stood in front of his seat and looked out at them, his eyes moving quickly from right to left, then slowly from left to right. He did not recognize any of the faces.

Within a few moments, some of the kids started exiting from the front of the bus. They smiled and said "good-bye" to the driver and slowly made their way down a couple of steps and out the door holding their paper bags or small suitcases or, in a few cases, both. A grown-up they recognized greeted them within seconds, sometimes right by the door of the bus. A few of them walked excitedly a few steps toward their mother or father or perhaps an aunt or another relative who would take them the rest of the way to their home in the city.

Luis continued looking out at the grownups, many of them with a kid beside them, on the sidewalk. He did not see his mother. He did not see his father. Nor did he see his grandmother or any other grownup he recognized. Suddenly, he was alone on the bus.

"Come on, it's time to get off," the bus driver said out to him. "Your mom is waiting for you."

Luis smiled, clutched the slightly ripped paper bag with his clothes and new toy, and walked to the front of the bus, down the steps, and out the door. He took a few steps on the sidewalk, and looked around as the bus started up and slowly drove away. He walked a few more steps and paused again to look around. The crowd of grownups and kids had begun dispersing and, in just a few more minutes, it seemed they were all gone. A few people walked by as they seem to do in all of the city's sidewalks. Luis looked around while standing by where dozens of grownups had just gathered to greet the kids that were on his bus. A few feet away, he saw a little boy holding a small suitcase, with a very sad look on his face. He looked like one of the other young boys who had just been on the bus with him. Luis took a few steps toward him.

"Hi," Luis said to the shorter and darker boy. "Are you waiting for your mom or dad?"

The boy looked at Luis and nodded, but said nothing. A tear began rolling down his left cheek.

"Oh, don't worry, they'll be here," Luis said, "I'm waiting for my mom, also. They'll all be here soon. Don't worry."

The two boys stood on the sidewalk holding their luggage for five minutes while people walked quickly by them. It was a hot summer day in lower

Manhattan, and by the shirts, pants and shoes they were wearing, Luis thought most of the people were going to work, or perhaps shopping. Some moved past the two of them slowly, with a dog on a leash. Five minutes became ten minutes, and then fifteen.

The little boy standing next to Luis began to cry. He put his suitcase down and started rubbing the eyes from where his tears were flowing, continuing to crying softly, "Mommy, daddy."

By this point, Luis was also on the verge of tears. As he stood in the middle of the sidewalk, he continued looking around him for a familiar face, but found none.

Finally, a white-haired woman with white-framed sunglasses wearing very nice clothes and strong perfume slowly approached the boys with a pronounced limp in her steps. She stopped less than a foot in front of them, tilted her head just a bit, and paused to look at the two sad kids.

"Hi boys, is something the matter?"

As soon as the words left her mouth, the little boy next to Luis blurted out, "My mommy and daddy! They're not here! I thought they would be here!"

The woman looked over at Luis.

"We just got back from being away," he began to explain. "The bus dropped a bunch of us off. Everyone left with their mom or dad except the two of us. We're the only ones still waiting."

The woman looked at the other boy and tried to tell him everything would be okay.

"They'll be here soon," she said. "Don't worry. Just wait a little longer."

But the little boy continued crying while she stood with them for a couple of minutes. Eventually, the woman began thinking the two boys might not be picked up by an adult anytime soon. She looked down at their sad faces, and noticed the suitcase by the little boy had a handwritten address on it. She bent down to read it, and recognized it as an uptown address a few miles away. She then looked at Luis and the large paper bag he was holding.

"Do you know where you live?"

"Yes, I do," he replied, nodding his head. "I live at 40 Amsterdam Avenue, apartment ten-bee."

The woman realized Luis lived uptown just a bit. She paused for a moment, looked inside her purse, then turned toward the two boys.

"How about a get a taxi to take both of you home?"

Luis raised his eyebrows. He had never been in a taxi, although he saw many of those yellow cars with a light on their roof drive by the street in front of his neighborhood. The other little boy looked up the woman, tears still streaming down his cheek, and nodded at her.

On a few of the evenings when he was in Pennsylvania, Luis enjoyed playing catch with Joseph and Joseph's father. Luis would borrow an old baseball glove that was a little small even for his small left hand, and try to catch a rubber ball with it that Joseph's father would alternate throwing to the two boys in the backyard while Joseph's mom prepared dinner in the kitchen. Luis had never used a baseball glove before, but he learned to catch the ball by using his right hand to secure it in his left hand. Throwing the ball back to Joseph's father was easy. By the end of his two weeks in Pennsylvania, catching the ball with the glove was also easy.

He never got used to the food Joseph's family ate for dinner, however. Almost every meal included potatoes and some kind of vegetable he did not care for. Most of them were green, but a few were white and one was even red. He always asked what kind of vegetable it was they wanted him to eat, and inevitably put a fork full of it in his mouth. Typically, he chewed the vegetable slowly, swallowed it, and with a pained look in his face would proclaim, "I really don't like it." The rest of the family found it amusing, and encouraged him to eat more of the vegetables by mixing them with potatoes or whatever else was on the plate. Luis did not, however, want to ruin the taste of any beef or chicken serving, which typically were much smaller than the amount of vegetables on his plate, by mixing them together.

When he explained to the Pennsylvania family that he ate a lot of different kinds of beans with rice at home, Joseph responded quizzically, "You eat a lot of red beans and black beans at home, but you don't want to eat green beans here?"

"We eat green beans sometimes," Luis replied, and proceeded trying to explain the green pigeon peas his mother referred to as *gandules* to the family. Joseph and his mother and father looked at him blankly, and continued eating their dinner.

A few minutes after the white-haired woman with the white-rimmed sunglasses had first talked to the two sad boys on the sidewalk, she limped toward the curb and hailed a yellow taxi driving slowly down the street. After the woman talked to the driver for a few moments, she backed away from the cab and it continued driving down the street. A minute later, she hailed another yellow taxi and again leaned into an open window to talk to the driver. She turned around and waved for the boys to come over.

"This cab will take you home," she explained. "He knows to stop at 40 Amsterdam Avenue first to drop you off," she said as she pointed at Luis, "and then he will continue uptown to take you home," she said to the shorter and darker boy. "You don't have to pay him."

Luis and the other boy smiled at the woman, and slowly climbed into the backseats of the yellow cab. Luis placed his brown bag on the floor in front of him, taking care not to rip it further. As the cab slowly pulled away, the woman smiled and waved at the two boys in the back.

Luis noticed the back seat of the taxi had a lot more room than the back seat of the car he rode with Joseph just a few hours earlier, when Joseph's mom had taken him to the bus station for the long ride home. It was very quiet outside the car on that ride, but Joseph and his mom could not stop talking inside of it. In the cab now, it was just the opposite. Luis could hear horns honking, jackhammers being used on pavement, and busses pulling away from their stops as the taxi headed north on Tenth Avenue. But inside the cab, Luis, the other boy and the driver said nothing. Everyone's eyes were focused on the activities outside.

When the taxi stopped for a red light on 60th street, Luis could see his apartment building just a block ahead on the left. He smiled and told the driver, "That's it, right there."

"I know," the cab driver replied. A moment later, the taxi pulled up alongside a parked car in front of Luis' apartment building. Luis assured the other boy that he, too, would also be home shortly. Luis closed the door, smiled at the boy and driver, and walked toward the front door of the building holding his shopping bag full of old and new clothes and toy. After he got inside, he walked past the mailboxes in the lobby and pushed the button for the elevator. The building's maintenance man smiled at him with a mouth full of missing teeth and mop in his hand. When Luis got inside the familiar elevator, he pushed the button next to the number "10." A moment later, he was in the hallway of the tenth floor. He walked to the door with the letter "B" in front and pushed the button to ring the bell. A few seconds later, he pushed the button again. His mother opened the door.

"Oh, hola. ¿Qué estás haciendo en casa?" ("Oh, hello. What are you doing home?")

Written in 2021.

About the author

Charles Lopez was born to Cuban immigrants who settled in New York City before the Revolution. After his parents divorced and he returned from an extended stay in Cuba, he began learning to speak English. Five years later his mother remarried, he moved to New Jersey and became known as Charles Bruns. He began working as a journalist while a teenager and launched his corporate communication career during college. Along the way, he married and raised a family. But he never stopped thinking about who he is and what he isn't or writing in his second language. Charles lives with his wife, Noreen, in Long Branch, New Jersey, where he continues writing about a wide range of topics in a variety of formats.

Shorts: Poems and Short Stories is Charles Lopez Bruns' third book. His memoir, *Fatherlands: Identities of a Cuban American,* was published in 2021 and is widely available online in print and digital formats. Charles' second book, *The Jersey Shore's First Luxury Condominium: A Hard-to-Believe History of Harbour Mansion*, based on a blog series he wrote, was published in 2023 and is available as a free e-book from Apple Books.

Front and back cover designs by Jim Redzinak.

Back cover photo of Charles in Cuba, November 1961, from Aunt Gloria Szwydky and Cousin Anna Iglesias.

Back cover photo of Charles in the United States, August 2025, by Noreen Bruns.

www.ingramcontent.com/pod-product-compliance
Lightning Source LLC
Chambersburg PA
CBHW051707180726
48283CB00004B/1240